To my friend and fellow writer, Jill Esbaum —PZM

For my two favorite little ducklings,
Henry & Hugo —DW

Library of Congress Cataloging-in-Publication Data:

Names: Miller, Pat Zietlow, author. | Wiseman, Daniel, illustrator.
Title: My brother the duck / by Pat Zietlow Miller ; illustrated by Daniel Wiseman.
Description: San Francisco : Chronicle Books, [2020] | Audience: Ages 3-5.
| Audience: Grades K-1. | Summary: Stella Wells, fledgling scientist, has a new baby brother, Drake,
and she is seriously considering the possibility that he is a duck—
but further research is required to test that hypothesis.
Identifiers: LCCN 2019026367 | ISBN 9781452142838 (hardback)
Subjects: LCSH: Infants—Juvenile fiction. | Brothers and sisters—Juvenile fiction. |
Ducks—Juvenile fiction. | Humorous stories. | CYAC:
Babies—Fiction. | Brothers and sisters—Fiction. | Ducks—Fiction. |
Humorous stories. | LCGFT: Humorous fiction.
Classification: LCC PZ7.M63224 My 2020 | DDC 813.6 [E]—dc23
LC record available at https://lccn.loc.gov/2019026367

Manufactured in China.

Design by Sara Gillingham Studio.
Handlettering by Daniel Wiseman. Typeset in Fela.
The illustrations in this book were rendered digitally.

10 9 8 7 6 5 4 3

Chronicle Books LLC
680 Second Street
San Francisco, California 94107

Chronicle Books—we see things differently.
Become part of our community at www.chroniclekids.com.

MY BROTHER THE DUCK

By PAT ZIETLOW MILLER   Illustrated by DANIEL WISEMAN

chronicle books·san francisco

I'm Stella Wells, fledgling scientist.
Scientists notice things, and so do I.

Like the fact my baby brother might be a duck.

I spotted something odd before he was born.
Dad told Mom: "You're waddling. We must be having a duck."

They laughed. I didn't.

A baby was bad enough.
A duck was unacceptable.
Research was obviously required.

So when my parents returned from the hospital holding something wrapped in a blanket, I took notes.

The thing was scrawny. It was yellow.
Its nose was flat and broad.
It looked like a duck.

But that was only a hypothesis.
To prove it, I'd need evidence.

Mom showed me
the bundle.

"Look, Stella, it's your
baby brother . . . Drake."

That name seemed noteworthy.

Turns out, "Drake" is a fancy word for a boy duck.
My first piece of evidence? Check.

As soon as I wrote it down, Drake started squawking.
Man, could that kid quack!

My second piece of evidence? Check.

LOUD QUACK? YES

• DRAKE?
IT MEANS
• BOY DUCK!

But scientists can't just wing it.
They have to gather facts.

TESTS:
☑ 1
☑ 2

So I visited my friend Carla Martinez.

She's made
volcanoes erupt,

pickles glow,

and paper clips float.

"We have a new baby. His name is Drake.
I think he's a duck."

Carla considered my statement. "Male ducks
are called drakes," she conceded. "Does he quack?"

"You should hear him."

"Does he have feathers?"

"Not yet. But he's fairly fuzzy."

"Does he have a bill?"

I stopped to think.
Drake's nose was definitely NOT normal.

"I guess so," I said.

Carla raised an eyebrow. "Scientists don't guess."

Further research was obviously required.

Back home, Drake looked more like a duck than ever.

"Incredible!" I said.

"But inconclusive," Carla replied. "We must consult an expert."

We chose Principal Kowalski.
She drinks coffee from a duck-shaped mug.
She keeps rubber ducks on her desk.

"Uh, Ms. Kowalski?" I said.
"We were wondering,
how can you tell
if a baby duck is, really,
you know, a duck?"

"You know what people say,
'If it looks like a duck
and sounds like a duck,
it's probably a duck.'"

There it was. An expert had
confirmed my hypothesis.
I was related to a duck.

A waddling, quacking,
broad-billed baby duck.

I thought about it all day.

Where we'd go. What we'd do. It wasn't so bad, really.

We could still go fishing.

We could still share lunch.

Drake's feathers would add a certain flair to every photo.

Plus, we'd never, ever, lose
a game of Duck, Duck, Goose.

I hurried home, ready to be
the best big sister a duck ever had.

Drake was in his bassinet.
He looked rounder and smoother than before.
His nose seemed almost . . . normal.

That didn't fit the bill.

Was all my research wrong? Just then, Dad waddled by.

I dropped my notebook and stared.

Long, skinny legs? Check.
Wide, webbed feet? Check.
The biggest bill I'd ever seen? Check.

"Pool time!" he announced.
"I need to get my wings wet!"

And with those words, I knew.

Stella Wells, fledgling scientist,
had another hypothesis to test.